To my husband and children for all their love and encouragement, to my parents for their support of my interest in science and meteorology, and to my weather education colleagues at **AMS** and **NOAA** for their thoughtful reviews of this book.

-Beth Mills

Weather wonders are all about.

Weather is awesome, there is no doubt.

It's a world of science exploration.

Come aboard the weather station!

Freddie the Front storms on through

Bringing colder or warmer air to you.

Clara the Cloud builds up high.

She sees people in planes soaring by.

Theo the Thunderstorm brings rain and winds.

Lightning and thunder he also sends.

Sometimes after Theo has passed by,

Renee the Rainbow appears in the sky.

Amazing weather happens in every season!

Isn't it cool to find out the reason?

In spring, Tony the Tornado often appears.

Knowledge and awareness can calm any fears.

In summer and fall, over the ocean,

Harriett the Hurricane is set into motion.

In winter, Sammie the Snowstorm spins up the coast

Bringing the big snows you like the most.

Weather wonders happen every day

All around the world in many a way.

The more you learn, the more can be shared

To help your family and friends be prepared!

Harriett the Hurricane

Copyright© 2014 by Beth Mills

Requests for permission to make copies of any part of the work should be submitted online at info@mascotbooks.com or mailed to Mascot Books, 560 Herndon Parkway #120, Herndon, VA 20170.

PRT0614A

Printed in the United States

Library of Congress Control Number: 2014908281
ISBN-13: 9781620866054

www.mascotbooks.com

Harriett the HURRICANE

Beth Mills

Illustrated by Casey Crisenbery

It was another muggy day over the tropical ocean
and the little cloud Harriett was bored.

"It's too quiet out here," Harriett said.

"I must find something fun to do."

She looked all around. Birds soared through
the air on their way to faraway places. Playful
dolphins jumped in and out of the warm ocean
waters below.

Harriett could not travel as far as the birds.

I cannot jump very high either, she thought.

Maybe I could try to spin.

Harriett took a deep breath and slowly twirled around.

"Wheeee! Look at me!"

She spun around until the birds and dolphins noticed her.

Harriett finally decided to stop and rest . . . but she couldn't!

Harriett's spinning created a strong wind blowing in a big circle over the ocean. The wind evaporated the warm ocean water. The water vapor condensed into clouds, and Harriett grew taller and wider.

I like being a bigger cloud, she thought.

Low air pressure formed at the center of Harriett and she became a tropical depression. This drew even more water vapor into Harriett. She spun faster and started to move westward. At first Harriett was very excited, but then she became a little scared.

"Oh no!" she exclaimed. "What do I do now?"

Harriett grew even larger and her winds became stronger. Harriett, who was once a little cloud, was now a tropical storm with winds blowing at least 39 miles per hour. Heavy rain fell from Harriett and the roar of her gusty winds made it hard to hear. As days passed, winds higher in the atmosphere continued to push her westward.

"I always wanted to see the world, but not like this," she sighed.

At last, Harriett brought in so much moisture from the ocean that she grew into a hurricane. Harriett had never felt so strong before, but she was worried. Birds and ships were avoiding her, moving away from her path.

Far in the distance, Harriett saw the green and brown
colors of land.

"I don't want to damage anything!" she cried.

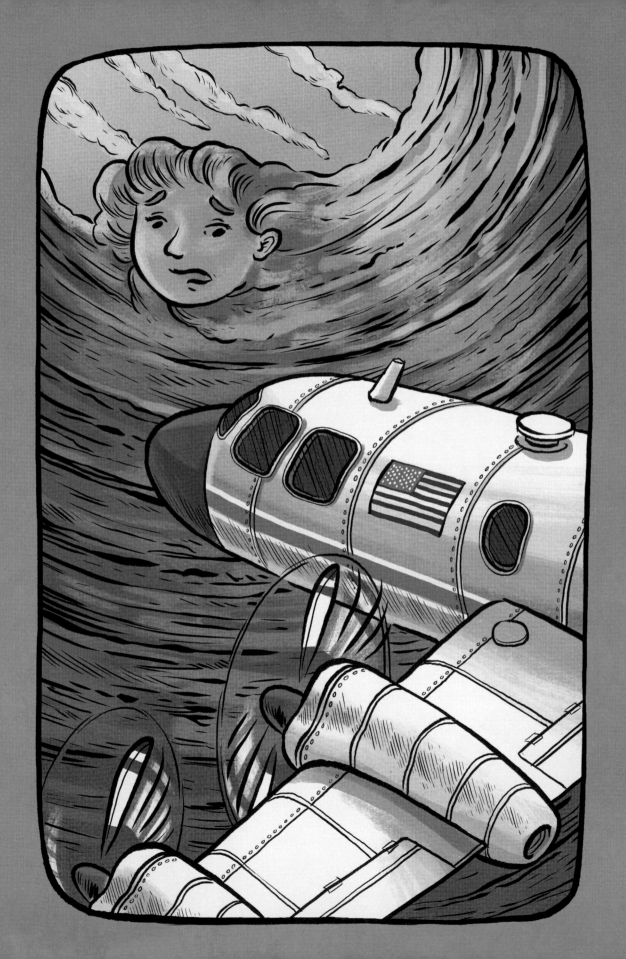

The next day when the sun rose, Harriett couldn't believe what she saw. An airplane was flying through her. This Hurricane Hunter dropped little packages of weather instruments. They measured conditions in her calm eye and surrounding eye wall where her winds were strongest.

Maybe I can talk to the people on the plane, she thought. They can warn those on the land.

Through the loud winds and pounding rain, Harriett yelled.

"Please let everyone know I'm coming! Please help them be prepared!"

The meteorologists contacted forecasters at the National
Hurricane Center in Miami, Florida.

"We definitely have a strong hurricane out here!"

"It confirms the satellite imagery you were examining.

She'll be making landfall in about two days."

The forecasters soon issued a hurricane watch for the areas Harriett could impact. When Harriett's landfall was a day and a half away, the forecasters issued hurricane warnings. People evacuated coastal areas and took shelter inland.

Meanwhile, Harriett wanted to slow her spinning.

Maybe I'll be lucky and move over cooler ocean water or bring in drier air, she thought.

But Harriett was running out of time. She could see the distant lights of coastal cities. Harriett was about to lose hope when she saw an undeveloped area of coastline.

"Please let me go that way!" she exclaimed.

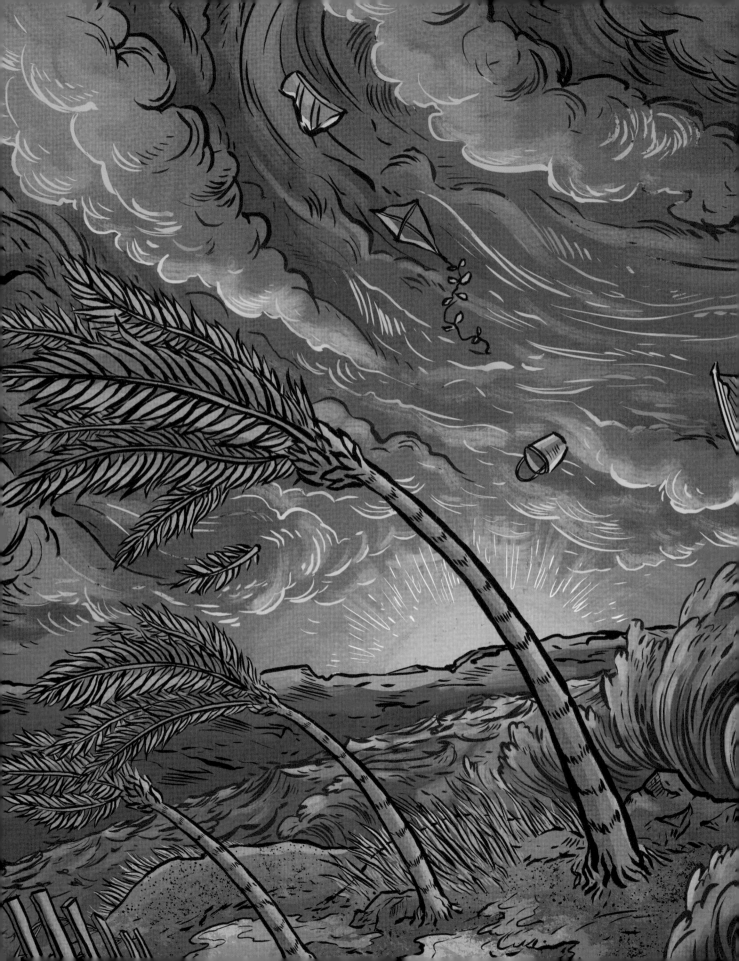

As Harriett approached the coast, the winds steering her shifted direction. As she made landfall, her eye wall just missed the cities. Her strong winds pounded the coastline. Harriett's storm surge and waves washed over the beaches and sand dunes. Trees swayed and branches snapped in the wind. Harriett's rains flooded coastal and inland areas.

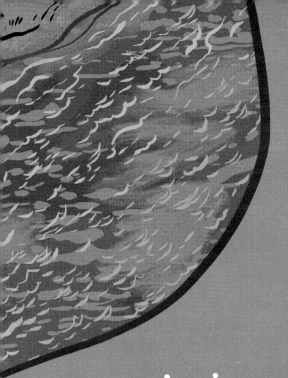

As Harriett moved inland, she breathed a sigh of relief.

"I'm not spinning so fast anymore. I'm starting to slow down," she rejoiced.

"People boarded up their houses and went into shelters. They listened to the forecasters!"

Harriett continued to weaken as she moved farther over the land because she didn't have energy from the warm ocean water to keep growing.

Finally, after all the adventure,
Harriett was a little cloud once more.

"What a ride!" exclaimed Harriett.

"But I will not try spinning again."

Glossary

Air Pressure – The force of the atmosphere on a unit area of Earth's surface. This force is the weight of the overlying air.

Atmosphere – The thin shell of gases and particles surrounding the Earth. The layer of the atmosphere closest to the ground is called the troposphere. Winds in the middle to upper troposphere direct the movement of a hurricane.

Condensation, Condense – The process of a gas becoming a liquid. Opposite of evaporation.

Evaporation, Evaporate – The process of a liquid becoming a gas. Opposite of condensation.

Eye – The circular core of light winds and calm weather at the center of a hurricane. The eye is surrounded by an eye wall.

Eye Wall – The ring of heavy rain and highest winds surrounding the eye of a hurricane.

Hurricane – A tropical low-pressure system with winds of 74 miles per hour or greater.

Hurricane Warning – A warning that hurricane conditions are expected in a certain coastal area, typically issued about 36 hours in advance so that people can prepare.

Hurricane Watch – An announcement that a hurricane poses a possible threat to certain coastal areas within 48 hours.

Moisture – The water vapor in the air, or the total water in the air (vapor, liquid, and solid).

National Hurricane Center – Office responsible for forecasting tropical cyclones in the Atlantic Basin, Gulf of Mexico, and the eastern tropical Pacific Ocean. Part of the National Oceanic and Atmospheric Administration.

Storm Surge – The mound of ocean water associated with a tropical storm or hurricane that can cause severe coastal flooding as the storm makes landfall.

Tropical Depression– An organized, tropical low-pressure system with surface winds of 38 miles per hour or less.

Tropical Storm – A tropical, low-pressure system with winds between 39 and 73 miles per hour.

Tropical Ocean – Portion of an ocean basin located in the tropics; between 23.5 degrees N and 23.5 degrees S latitude. Hurricanes form at least a few hundred miles north or south of the Earth's equator over warm ocean waters (at least 80 °F).

Water Vapor – Water in the form of a gas.

Further Information

Harriett the Hurricane explores the wonder many feel about the weather. It also emphasizes safety and the need to be aware and prepare.

Tropical storms and hurricanes are extremely dangerous. They cause high winds, heavy rainfall, coastal and inland flooding, and tornadoes. Often heavy rains occur over areas far from where the storm makes landfall. It is very important to prepare and plan with your family before hurricane season begins. If you are in a watch or warning area, follow the directions of local authorities. The safety of your family is always most important!

The National Oceanic and Atmospheric Administration's (NOAA) National Weather Service (NWS) is responsible for tropical storm and hurricane forecasts. The NOAA National Hurricane Center issues watches and warnings. Local forecast offices give detailed information for where you live.

Great online sources of information are:
National Hurricane Center: www.nhc.noaa.gov
NWS Hurricane Preparedness: www.nws.noaa.gov/om/hurricane
Federal Emergency Management Agency: www.ready.gov/hurricanes
American Red Cross: www.redcross.org
The Young Meteorologist Program: www.youngmeteorologist.org/game/index.html

You can be a member of the American Meteorological Society!
Are you fascinated by weather and want to learn more? K-12 students can become AMS associate members and receive a subscription to *Weatherwise* magazine or the *Bulletin of the American Meteorological Society*. Visit www.ametsoc.org/MEMB/ for more information.

Opportunities for Teachers
The AMS Education Program offers semester-long professional development courses in weather, water, and climate for in-service K-12 teachers through its national DataStreme program. Visit www.ametsoc.org/amsedu for details.

About the Author

Beth Mills is a meteorologist who has worked in science education for more than a decade. She helps train K-12 teachers nationwide in topics of weather, ocean, and climate, and designs college-level Earth science courses.

Beth holds B.S. and M.S. in Meteorology degrees from Penn State University. Her interest in weather started in elementary school after she witnessed two tropical storms while traveling in the South.

Beth is passionate about helping young people explore careers in atmospheric and related sciences. She believes that weather is an excellent way to introduce kids to science, opening doors for further exploration.